READ ALL OF
AXEL & BEAST'S
ADVENTURES!

AXEL & BEAST

THE GRABBEM GETAWAY

ADRIAN C. BOTT ART BY ANDY ISAAC

Kane Miller
A DIVISION OF EDC PUBLISHING

First American Edition 2017
Kane Miller, A Division of EDC Publishing

Text Copyright © Adrian C Bott 2016
Illustration Copyright © Andy Isaac 2016
First published in Australia by Hardie Grant Egmont 2016

For information contact:
Kane Miller, A Division of EDC Publishing
P.O. Box 470663
Tulsa, OK 74147-0663
www.kanemiller.com
www.edcpub.com
www.usbornebooksandmore.com

Library of Congress Control Number: 2016955648

Printed and bound in the United States of America
9 10 11 12 13 14 15

ISBN: 978-1-61067-633-5

To our little Bean,
who helped me find the stories.

CHAPTER 1

If a secret agent had gone to Axel Brayburn's little house in the suburbs, he would have given Axel a job on the spot.

"Here's your laser-cutter pen, your exploding chewing gum, the keys to your customized motorbike and a brand-new bow tie," the agent would have said. "Oh, and don't forget your shiny black secret-agency membership card. One edge is sharp, so you can use it to cut through ropes, or shave with it once you're old enough."

Axel was **definitely** spy material, though he didn't know it himself. Despite only being twelve years old, Axel had plenty of the qualities a secret agent needs: fast reactions, common sense, technical savvy, and even some judo training. His eyesight was the only problem – he needed thick glasses – but a few million dollars' worth of advanced laser treatment and cyber implants could have fixed that.

Of course, secret agents don't just go around to people's houses to give them jobs, and Axel was just a regular twelve-year-old. He had no idea that he'd make a good spy. So far as he knew, there was only one thing his skills made him *really* good at.

Video games.

There were two players left in the game he was playing that morning. Victory was so close, Axel was trembling all over.

He steered his little Tankinator – a robot tank that looked like a trash can on wheels – into the safety of a cave. Now he could lie low for a few seconds and recover some energy.

Axel played a lot of online games like *Tankinator Arena*. Especially in the middle of the day, with the curtains drawn, like now.

Anyone could play the game, but the best Tankinators cost real money, and they were more powerful. That meant you could be a super-skilled player like Axel, but still lose against someone with plenty of money.

Axel's opponent, BAGGER_63, was clearly **rolling** in money. He'd bought the biggest, shiniest Tankinator money could buy. It had armor like a battleship, dozens of special features and more weapons than a Christmas tree has lights.

But Axel had *almost* beaten him – first by encouraging all the other players to team up against him, and then by cleverly using the terrain to hide, fire and hide again. Now BAGGER_63 had only a tiny bit of health left.

Cautiously, Axel peeped out of the cave … only to find he was looking right down the barrel of BAGGER_63's main cannon.

BOOM! Axel's health bar vanished in a split second.

"Arrr!" he yelled, as his little Tankinator exploded into a fireball of pixels.

"Owned again!" came BAGGER_63's voice through Axel's headphones.

BAGGER_63 drove his enormous elite Tankinator back and forth over the **smoldering** remains of Axel's tiny one, grinding them into the dirt.

"How did you find me?" yelled Axel.

"I have top-of-the-line scanners, **fool.** Worth every penny I paid for them!"

The end-of-round display flashed up. It showed BAGGER_63 at the top of the leaderboard, and AX-MAN just below.

No prize for second place. No reward at all.

"You want to try beating me with a regular Tankinator?" Axel raged. "Maybe try using, I don't know, actual *skill* instead of just buying stuff?"

"Cry more, noob!" came the smug reply. There was a brief blast of thrash metal music.

Axel said nothing. He quit the game, pulled his headphones off and sat on the end of his bed, staring at the blank screen.

He didn't own an elite Tankinator because he couldn't afford one. Axel didn't get much allowance. What little money his mom earned as a mechanic went toward food, bills and more bills. His game console was the most expensive thing he owned. It had been last year's birthday present from his dad, before what had happened … had happened.

His mother, Nedra, knocked. "Oh, Axel, you'll ruin your eyesight, that close to the screen!"

Axel tapped his thick glasses. "Don't think it can get much worse than it is, Mom."

"Planning on staying in all day again?"

Axel shrugged.

"It's lovely outside," said his mom.

"That's nice."

Nedra sighed. "Oh well. Have fun. I'm going to fix Mr. Cornish's lawn mower."

"Good luck!"

"You, too. I'll only be half an hour. Try not to wreck the place."

No chance of that, Axel thought. *I probably won't even leave this room.*

He fired up *Tankinator Arena* again, went to the game's store section and looked longingly at all the amazing gear you could buy.

Vehicles with superpowered weapons, speed boosts, extra armor, even custom paint jobs. All for a price, of course. He lost track of time as he daydreamed about what it must feel like to own an elite Tankinator ...

KA-THOOM!

It was the sound of a big metal object being crashed through. Just like when his little Tankinator got shot. Only louder.

Axel leapt to his feet.

The next moment, the screen went black.

Axel's first thought was: *What* was *that noise? It didn't come from the game!*

His second thought was: *Did we blow a fuse? The power's gone out.*

"Dad?" he said aloud, then felt silly for saying it. His father had gone missing a year ago, when he'd gone to pick up some takeout and had never come back. There had been no news since then, not even a whisper. But all the same ...

From downstairs came the creak and groan of metal being bent out of shape.

Axel left his room and cautiously crept down the stairs. The light in the hallway flickered. He noticed his mom's favorite Buddha statue – a present from her own mother in Sri Lanka – had fallen off the hall table. He quickly put it back and then headed for the inside door that led to the garage.

From behind the door came odd noises. **Wheeze-clunk. Wheeze-clunk.**

"This is deeply weird," Axel said to himself.

He hesitated, wondering if he should wait for his mom to come home before finding out what was going on.

No, he thought. *I'm twelve. She left me in charge. I can handle this, whatever it is ...*

He flung the door open and leapt inside the garage with a yell.

The yell turned into a **gasp.**

The metal garage door – what was left of it – had been crumpled up like a bit of aluminum foil. But even stranger than that, something had tried to flatten it out again. It stood jammed into the gap where it had once hung, a battered, sorry-looking mess.

A **large robot** was standing there, looking at him.

It had an electrical cord dangling from where its mouth would have been if it had one, almost like it was sucking on a bit of licorice. Blue sparks flew.

It looked guilty. When it saw Axel, it jumped.

It **jumped.**

Axel stood paralyzed, not sure what to do.

Part of him wanted to scream. Another part wanted to burst out laughing because he was obviously going crazy, and that meant he could take his clothes off and empty **baked beans** over his head and do other sorts of crazy things. But what he actually did surprised him.

"It's okay!" Axel said, holding his hands out. "I won't hurt you."

The robot's shoulders sagged in relief.

Axel took a good look at it. He wasn't imagining it, and he wasn't dreaming. It was quite real: a chunky green-and-black robot over six feet tall, with panels all over it that things probably came out of, like tools or guns maybe. In its chest was a faintly transparent canopy, covering a padded small-person-sized hole.

Somebody me-sized can climb inside this

robot, Axel realized. He glimpsed some tempting-looking controls inside the chest, too. Maybe it was meant to be operated from within. *What would happen if I tried?*

Axel took a step forward. The robot watched him with big, unblinking eyes.

"Are you … an alien?"

The robot shook its head. **Whizz-whizz** went the mechanisms in its neck.

"Can you speak?"

The robot nodded. It looked up at the mangled garage door, then back to Axel.

"SORRY," it said. Its voice was electronic, exactly like Axel expected it to sound. "DOOR BROKE."

"Yes," echoed Axel. "Door *very* broke."

"TRIED TO FIX IT," the robot said. It hung its head, looking as sorry as a guilty dog.

Axel remembered his mother's words. *"Don't wreck the place ..."* A chill went through him. She was going to lose it.

The robot dropped the power cord and let out a digital **buuuurp,** which sounded like an old-fashioned phone. The garage light went on, but weakly.

"Have you been eating our electricity?" Axel demanded.

The robot shuffled away from him. "SORRY," it said again. "HUNGRY."

"What are you even *doing* here?"

The robot huddled itself into a ball.

"BEAST IS HIDING," it said.

"That's your name? Beast?"

Another nod.

"It's okay. I understand. Hiding is the right thing to do sometimes," said Axel.

BEAST looked at him.

There was a pause. Very slowly, BEAST uncurled itself until it was standing up.

Axel took a breath. "I'm Axel, by the way. I like hiding, too."

"WHERE?"

"Oh. All sorts of places. Mostly I used to hide in the old supply closet at school. Nobody ever found me." Axel made a face. "Once I stayed in there for so long they locked the school up and went home. Mom went pretty crazy over that."

BEAST thought about that. "WHO WAS AXEL HIDING FROM?"

"Bigger kids. So long as you only have to fight one bully at a time, you can fight. I fought a *lot*. But when they start jumping you in a gang, you kind of have to hide."

"IS CLOSET A GOOD HIDING PLACE?"

"The best," said Axel. "Especially if you

brought a book."

BEAST nodded. It held out a huge robotic hand. "PLEASE TAKE BEAST TO **SUPPLY CLOSET.**"

"Uh. I can't," Axel said.

"PLEASE."

"No!"

"BUT BEAST NEEDS TO HIDE. HE AND AXEL CAN HIDE TOGETHER."

"You don't understand. I can't take you there. I don't go to that school anymore. Or any school." Axel paused. This part was always hard to explain. "I'm homeschooled. Mom teaches me now. Because of all the fighting. And the hiding."

BEAST was still holding its – no, *his*, thought Axel – hand out. The robot was trembling and his eyes had gotten very big. Axel didn't understand how something so big could look so frightened.

"So who are you hiding from?" he asked.

Before BEAST could reply, there was a scream from outside. It was his mother's voice. She was back from fixing Mr. Cornish's lawn mower.

"Axel?" she yelled. "Where are you? *Axel!* Answer me! **What on earth has happened to our house?"**

CHAPTER

Axel thought fast. "This way," he told BEAST, and ran through the door back into the house.

BEAST crammed himself through the door. He was too big to fit, but he pushed his way through anyway. Axel winced at the sound of **splintering wood.**

Through the glass in the front door he could see his mother at the top of the driveway. She was yelling something about **property damage.** Now she was coming toward the front door, her keys in her hand.

"Upstairs! Hurry!"

Axel sprinted up to his bedroom door. BEAST crashed up behind him, the stairs cracking underfoot as he went. *He's like a dog*, Axel thought. *A huge daft dog that doesn't know how big he is.*

Axel pointed BEAST into his bedroom. The robot had to hunker all the way down to get through the door, but just about managed it. With a **donk,** Axel's model spaceship fell from his bedside table. BEAST trod on it.

A key turned in the front door lock. The door opened.

"Axel?" his mother called, sounding desperate. "Just tell me you're safe!"

"I'm fine, Mom!"

It was rapidly dawning on Axel that a giant robot in your bedroom isn't any easier to explain away than a giant robot in your garage, but it was too late to change his mind now. He could think of only one thing to do.

He grabbed the sheets from his bed and threw them over BEAST.

He could hear his mom coming up the stairs. "What's happening? Where are you?"

"Having a nap!" Axel yelled.

"**DARK ENVIRONMENT DETECTED.** ENGAGING NIGHT-VISION MODE," said BEAST from under the sheets.

"**What was that?**" screeched Axel's mother. "Who's in there?"

"It's just my video game!" Axel said.

The bedroom door flew open. His mother stood there, breathing hard, with oil on her fingers and a **terrible** look on her face.

"Did you fix the lawn mower?" Axel asked innocently.

"Never mind the lawn mower," his mom yelled. "Explain to me why the garage door is wrecked, along with the stairs! Surely you noticed?"

"Um, not really. I had the volume up pretty loud."

"And what's this?" She jabbed a finger at the huge mound of sheets.

Axel's sheets slowly slid off BEAST's head. The robot looked up at Axel's mother, who was opening and closing her mouth like a goldfish.

"HELLO," said BEAST.

"..." said Axel's mother.

"He's a robot," Axel said. "I, uh, won him in a competition, and the delivery men couldn't get him in the front door, so they had to take the garage door off, and they broke it, and, and, and ..."

His mom held up a hand to shush him. "I am going to get us all some milk and cookies," she said in a shaking voice, "and then we can have a nice sit-down and a chat. Okay?"

"Okay," said Axel.

"OKAY," said BEAST.

Ten minutes later, Axel and Nedra were sitting on the bed, while BEAST held a tiny cookie in his enormous clawlike hand. The robot glanced around as if he were very nervous.

"He's called BEAST," explained Axel.

"STANDS FOR **BATTLE-ENABLED ARMORED SHIFTER TRANSPORT,**" said BEAST, and Axel thought he sounded proud of himself for once. Then Axel thought: *What does* **shifter** *mean?*

"Why were you hiding in our garage?" asked Axel's mother, who had calmed down a bit.

"DON'T WANT TO GO BACK," said BEAST. "BAD MEN WANTED ME TO **DESTROY** NICE THINGS."

"Nice things? Like what?"

"TREES," said BEAST. "FLOWERS. CORAL. PRETTY HILLS."

"I don't understand," said Axel.

"I do," said his mother. She sounded angry again. "Look at the symbol on BEAST's chest."

Axel hadn't noticed the little symbol until she pointed it out. It was a red G that looked like a clenched fist.

"That symbol stands for the greediest, sneakiest, wickedest corporation in the world," she hissed through her teeth. "They're always on the news, sliming their way out of one investigation or another. There's no other corporation out there that breaks the law and gets away with it so often."

"You mean … **Grabbem Industries?**" said Axel.

At the mention of Grabbem Industries, BEAST tried to hide under Axel's bed and there was chaos for a moment, since Axel and his mom were **still sitting on it.** But they soon settled BEAST back down.

"They're bad people, Axel," his mom said. "They have billions of dollars already and they want even more, and they don't care how much of the environment they rip up to get it."

"So? That doesn't mean BEAST is bad!"

Axel's mother looked at him very seriously. "This robot is a weapon. It said it was *battle* enabled. It's dangerous."

"BEAST's not an *it*, he's a **he.** And he isn't dangerous!" yelled Axel. "Didn't you hear him? He doesn't *want* to destroy things.

That's why he ran away!"

"I'm sorry, Axel. Grabbem Industries are going to be out looking for him. We have to tell them where he is, or they'll want to know why we didn't. And this family's already been through enough."

BEAST trembled.

Nedra stood up and headed for the door. Axel dived into her path and stood in the doorway, blocking it.

"Don't make him go back, Mom!" Axel begged.

She looked at BEAST and back to Axel, held up her hands, and sighed. "What other choice do I have?"

A strange, deep voice said, "I think perhaps I can help with that."

Axel and his mom looked over to where the voice was coming from. BEAST had stopped moving and his eyes had rolled upward. A beam of misty blue light was shining out of BEAST's chest. At its end, it formed a 3-D image of a tall man with dark glasses, hunched over his desk.

"A hologram projector!" said Axel.

The man nodded. "Correct. I am a friend. You may call me Agent Omega. It is very important that you listen to what I have to say."

"And why is it so important?" demanded Axel's mother.

"Because in just under five minutes, Grabbem Industries are going to **attack your house!**"

CHAPTER 3

The headquarters of Grabbem Industries, where the Grabbem family lived, was a gigantic mansion made of steel and glass.

Beneath the mansion, running far underground, were gloomy offices and factories and tunnels and secret laboratories. Down there, thousands of people worked for Grabbem, toiling away like termites in a mound. They never got to see the sun, but Mr. Grabbem liked it this way. It meant he didn't have to look at them.

The mansion looked like it was beside a lake, but it wasn't. What looked like a lake at first sight was actually the most enormous swimming pool in the world. Hundreds of people worked every night to keep it clean, but only three people ever got to swim in it, and it was so big they only ever swam around in one tiny corner, which made the whole thing completely pointless. Those three people were Mr. Grabbem, his wife and their **horrible son,** Gus Junior.

The sun shone bright. All the Grabbems grumbled. They hated the outdoors, but they believed all rich people were expected to sit outside in the sun by their enormous swimming pools every day, whether they liked it or not. So that was what they did.

At this moment, Mr. Grabbem and his wife were sitting in deck chairs and Gus Grabbem was jumping up and down.

"I don't want any **lousy breakfast,** I want my robot back!" yelled Gus.

"You'll get it back," snapped Mr. Grabbem. "I just sent two of my top people out to fetch it."

Mr. Grabbem was rich. He was so rich he sometimes wiped his nose with money, just because he could. Outside the house were a hundred dumpsters full of the toys he'd bought for Gus, which had all been broken the same day.

Right now, Mr. Grabbem was wearing board shorts and sunglasses and a bright-red sunburn, which made his bad mood even worse.

"I want it back *now*!" yelled Gus. "It's not fair. I never even got to fly around in it!"

Gus, who was thirteen, was wearing a bunny suit covered in splashes of red paint. This was because he was pretending to be something called **Roadkill Rabbit** from one of his nasty horror comics.

"Oh, precious, you didn't really want to do something so dangerous, did you?" said Mrs. Grabbem, whose skin was a very odd orange color from too much fake tan. "Go sit in your racing car instead. Where's your racing car?"

"Drove it into a tree," said Gus.

"The BEAST project isn't dangerous, Shona," said Mr. Grabbem irritably. "The whole point of the **robot suit** was to keep young Gus safe while he blows stuff up for the company."

"Kaboom," shouted Gus. ***"Whoosh. Vreeeow."***

If there was one thing Gus Grabbem Junior

loved, it was smashing stuff up. Or burning it. Or slicing it up with chainsaws.

Mr. Grabbem had become rich by getting minerals and oil and gems out of the ground, and most of the time that meant getting rid of what was in his way. He cut down forests, blasted open hills and blew up mountains, which made Gus jealous because *he* wanted to do that sort of thing.

So Mr. Grabbem had asked his scientists to make a special armored robot suit for Gus, with dozens of weapons built into it. But the suit had disappeared that very morning.

Mr. Grabbem's phone rang. It was the size of a postage stamp and had cost ten thousand dollars. Because it was so small and fiddly, he nearly dropped it in the pool when answering it.

"Yes?"

"This is Alpha One. We have located BEAST," said a crackly voice. "Attempting recovery now."

"About time. Get that robot back here on the double. And if it won't come – blow it to pieces."

"Sir, are you sure? It cost so much …"

"I don't pay you to think. Do as you're told." Mr. Grabbem angrily hung up the phone and lost his grip on it. It fell in the pool. He shrugged and went indoors to order an even smaller, more expensive phone.

Meanwhile, deep below the mansion, below the factory floors and the rooms full of science equipment, there was a tunnel where hardly anyone ever went. At the end of the tunnel, under a flickering light, was a room where *nobody at all* ever went.

Except for one man.

His real name was Cedric Bunk, but he called himself Agent Omega. Although he worked for Grabbem Industries, he hated everything about them. He was determined to smash them from the inside.

Right now he was sitting at a computer, talking to Axel and his mother via holographic projection.

"Listen carefully. There are two Grabbem fighter craft closing in on your location. They are armed with rapid-fire, high-explosive missiles. You have only two options. One is to surrender."

"What's the other?" said Axel.

"Fight, of course."

"Erm … are you sure?" Axel fingered his glasses nervously. "I've only fought Tankinators and stuff before. You do know they're not real, right?"

"Your gaming skills will be more useful than you think," Agent Omega said urgently. "In fact –"

"I can't believe I'm hearing this!" Axel's mother yelled. "What do you mean, *fight*? How can he fight them? He's only twelve!"

Agent Omega noticed a blinking light on his computer. He had just a few moments left before the Grabbem security systems detected what he was doing.

"BEAST is powerful, but he's helpless without a pilot. That's where you come in, Axel. You'll have to get inside BEAST and **fly him into battle.** It's your only chance!"

CHAPTER 4

"No," said Nedra.

"But, *Mom* ..."

She pointed a **furious finger** at Agent Omega. "How dare you? This is my son. I won't have you putting him in danger."

BEAST looked up at the ceiling. He was trembling, as if he expected something bad to come crashing through it.

Axel made up his mind. "Tell me what I need to know," he said.

"I've only got a few seconds left before they detect me," said Agent Omega, "so listen carefully. BEAST has a **tracking device** buried deep inside of him."

"Got it," said Axel.

"Grabbem will be able to track him anywhere, for as long as he remains above ground. The only way to stop them ..."

Agent Omega's image vanished suddenly, like a candle flame being blown out.

"I guess they detected him," said Axel hollowly.

BEAST lowered his head back down, looked at Axel and blinked, like he was waking up from a nap.

Axel's mom took a deep breath. "BEAST, I'm sorry, but I need you to leave. **Right now.** Go as far away from the house as you can."

"No," Axel yelled, but BEAST had already

begun to trudge out of the room and down the stairs. He looked sadly over his shoulder.

Nedra grabbed Axel's arm. "Let him go."

"But he's in trouble!"

"You heard what that Omega man said. Grabbem can track him anywhere. Don't you see? If he stays here, it'll be us who are in trouble. Ever since your dad disappeared … "

From overhead came a distant roaring sound, like a **low-flying plane.** Axel expected it to pass, but it grew steadily louder.

"That's them," he said. "They're coming."

BEAST was carefully opening the front door and squeezing himself through it.

Axel pulled out of his mother's grasp and ran after him. "Wait," he yelled.

"Axel," his mom shouted. "I'm warning you! Get back inside *right now* …"

Axel caught up with the robot outside the

house. He pulled at the transparent panel on BEAST's chest, hoping it would open. It did. The clear panel lifted easily out of the way.

Before Nedra could catch up, Axel had clambered inside the soft hollow. His hands found the controls and a harness slipped easily over his chest.

The canopy slid shut in front of him and the view through the transparent panel suddenly went blurry, as if they were going through a car wash. Lights flickered before Axel's eyes, and the message **OPTIC SCAN COMPLETE** appeared and vanished. The view snapped back into perfect focus. And then:

"Oh, man," Axel breathed.

It was like stepping into a new world.

Wherever he looked, the view was magnified. He could see *everything*.

Every leaf on every tree stood out in perfect

detail. He concentrated his attention on one leaf, and the view zoomed in as if BEAST had read his mind. He stared at the grit on the driveway until it looked like boulders. Reality had become high definition.

But he wasn't just seeing the world. BEAST's senses were **reading** the world, too. Wherever he looked, tiny letters made of light told him what everything he could see was made of. The longer he focused on something, the more information appeared.

Axel stared at a tree branch, reading the information that scrolled past. He learned it was an elm, thirty years old, slightly unhealthy because of car exhaust, damaged in a storm once but doing fine now. An image of the tree's DNA appeared, a corkscrew spiral turning around and around.

As well as telling Axel what everything

around was made of, the writing also showed what BEAST could do with it. The front door was **WOOD (BREAKABLE),** the ground was **EARTH (DIGGABLE).** Nedra's car, parked at the top of the driveway, could be **EASILY LIFTED.**

I could pick up my mom's car right now, Axel thought giddily. *And probably throw it into the air and catch it, too.* He felt superhuman.

Axel took a few steps. He held one of BEAST's arms up in front of his face and wiggled the thick robot fingers. This was incredible. He had total control.

"BEAST, I think I can do this. Let's get moving," he said.

Nedra came running out of the house, tears in her eyes. "Why are you so stubborn? Just like your dad. I can't lose you, too!"

"I've got to stop them, Mom." Axel's voice

sounded strange coming out of BEAST's speakers.

She hung her head. "Just promise me you'll look after each other, okay?"

"I PROMISE," said BEAST.

"Me, too," said Axel.

Nedra's long black hair blew in the wind. She looked up. Two tiny specks had appeared in the sky.

"Good luck, mate," she said hoarsely. "I love you."

Agent Omega had said Axel should fly BEAST into battle. "BEAST?" Axel said. "Take us up."

What happened next was like stepping into an elevator, pressing the button for the top floor expecting a gentle ride up, and then being fired from a cannon.

Axel yelled as BEAST rocketed upward. His

innards felt like they were being forced down into his feet. **"Whoaaaaaaa!"**

After a few seconds, he looked down. Trails of white exhaust were spiraling from BEAST's feet.

Below them was a view of his hometown he'd only ever seen before on Google Maps. The roads were just a pale-gray crisscross of lines from up here. There was the little cluster of shops, and there was the town hall, shaped like a big T. He could even see the green sports fields at the school.

"This is amazing," he breathed.

"YOUR HEART RATE IS EXTREMELY FAST," warned BEAST.

Axel reminded himself they weren't there to sightsee. "Okay. Where are the Grabbem craft Agent Omega told us about?"

BEAST popped up a display. It showed two

attack ships swerving and coasting through the sky. They looked like flat crabs, each one equipped with a strong pair of mechanical pincers. They skimmed through the clouds like stones skipped across the water, except much deadlier.

"How long till they reach us?"

"TEN SECONDS," said BEAST.

"What?"

"**CORRECTION.** NINE SECONDS. **CORRECTION.** EIGHT SECONDS ..."

"Give me manual flight control," Axel said desperately.

"OKAY." Something like a balloon swelled up under Axel's left hand. "WOULD YOU LIKE TO CONSULT THE FLIGHT CONTROL INSTRUCTION BOOK?"

"There isn't time. Just let me fly!"

Axel squeezed the balloon thing hard.

The sudden **thooom** of acceleration nearly drove his head into his neck. He let go.

"That's the throttle, then," he gasped. "Now how do I steer – a-ha!" Under his right hand was a rolling ball that moved a set of crosshairs in his field of view.

Guessing that he could choose his direction with one hand and his speed with the other, Axel tried aiming at the horizon and giving the throttle a gentler squeeze.

He went thundering through the sky like an armored missile. Clouds swept past. The skyline shook as air resistance buffeted them.

"So far, so good," Axel gasped. "I can do this."

Meanwhile, the two Grabbem pilots were confused.

"What do we do now?" said the first pilot, Alpha One.

"We go after him, *duh*," said the second pilot, Alpha Gold.

The pilots had argued earlier about which of them should be Alpha One and which had to be Alpha Two. Alpha One had eventually won because he was oldest, upon which Alpha Two had changed his name to Alpha Gold.

Alpha One had said that wasn't allowed because it was meant to be numbers, and Alpha Gold had replied that he didn't care, he could be colors if he wanted. Alpha One had shouted that it wasn't fair because Alpha Gold sounded even cooler than Alpha One. Alpha Gold had said **ha-ha-ha,** he was stuck with it now.

"In pursuit!" said Alpha One. He fired his thrusters and tore through the clouds after BEAST.

"Also in pursuit!" said Alpha Gold.

He went to fire his own thrusters and accidentally fired a missile instead. It streaked through the air and off into the distance.

"Watch what you're doing!" screamed Alpha One.

Up ahead, Axel saw the missile whizz past.

"Oh, no," he said. "BEAST, I don't think they're trying to capture you anymore. They're trying to blow us up!"

CHAPTER 5

"BEAST IS SCARED," said BEAST.

"Don't worry, BEAST," said Axel, though his own heart was **pounding.** "We're going to make it through this together. Trust me."

"YOU ARE BEAST'S PILOT, AXEL. OF COURSE BEAST TRUSTS YOU," said BEAST.

The two Grabbem ships were right on their tail.

Time to stand and fight, thought Axel. *I'm a gamer. I've been in situations like this a thousand times. I just have to trust my skills.*

Luckily, they were high above the ground and pretty far from the nearest town, so they could have a fight without any bystanders getting hurt.

"Let's do this. BEAST, what are you armed with?" he asked.

"ARMED?"

Axel blinked. **"Weapons.** What **weapons** have you got?"

"NONE."

Axel's heart felt like it had just fallen out of his body. Suddenly he didn't feel like the luckiest kid in the world, piloting an amazing robot through the clouds. He felt like a small boy trapped in what might as well be a rocket-powered refrigerator.

"No **weapons** at all?" he yelled.

"OFFENSIVE CAPABILITIES ARE AVAIL-ABLE IN MY OTHER FORMS. YOU WILL NEED **APPS** TO ACCESS THEM."

Apps?

Before Axel could figure out what on earth BEAST was talking about, there was a red flash from behind and a whooshing, hissing noise. A blaring alarm went off inside BEAST's head.

A message box lit up: **missile locked on.**

Axel reacted instantly, without pausing to think. He threw BEAST into a power dive, aiming for the ground.

A camera view of the oncoming missile appeared in the corner of his vision, shaking around wildly.

The surface beneath them was brownish green and uneven looking. It was the tops of trees, bumpy with leaves. They were flying down toward a huge stretch of forest.

Axel swerved hard to the left, hoping the missile wouldn't be able to turn as quickly as BEAST. It came around in a **whooshing loop** and was right back on their trail again.

"Can't shake him," Axel muttered through clenched teeth. "Can you go any faster?"

"NOT IN THIS FORM," said BEAST, sounding gloomy.

"So what are you waiting for? Change form!"

"ALTERNATE FORMS ARE AVAILABLE, BUT YOU WILL NEED **APPS** TO ACCESS THEM."

"And I don't have any **apps**," Axel finished. "Fine. I get it."

He wove in a series of wild S-bends, just clipping the tops of the forest trees. The missile followed, getting closer every second, never slowing.

It was going to blow them out of the sky, and there was nothing Axel could do about it. Without these all-important **apps** it seemed BEAST was helpless. Why hadn't Agent Omega warned him? He knew this would be a crazy risk ...

"A crazy risk," Axel breathed.

He raised BEAST's fists in front of him, superhero style, and deliberately flew down into the green forest.

Breaking through the forest canopy was like being attacked by mad wood goblins. Branches battered him like clubs. Sticks thwacked across BEAST's head. Leaves whipped into his face. Axel yelled out loud. BEAST went out of control, flailing and tumbling.

The world **spun around and around** sickeningly. Axel grabbed the controls and forced BEAST back into a straight, level flight path. They were now flying only a few feet above the forest floor, and they were volleying in between thick tree trunks that rushed past like the pillars of highway bridges.

There was only a tiny amount of space to squeeze through.

A broad oak **loomed** up, right in their path. They were flying so fast that Axel barely had time to swerve out of the way. If he'd hit the tree, they would have been crushed to a pulp.

The **missile locked on** box began flashing a brilliant red.

"Okay," Axel said, "it's still coming. I just hope this works."

He weaved in and out of the trees, looking for one that would suit what he had in mind. There, up ahead, was a tall tree that looked ideal. He powered toward it, the missile only inches behind.

The tree loomed large in his vision.

Axel pulled BEAST up, racing along the entire length of the tree, skimming the trunk. Below them, the missile tilted to follow – but not fast enough. It hit the tree.

An astonishing **fireball** blossomed beneath them. The next second, the shockwave hit, throwing them farther into the air. With a long, sad groan, the tree slowly toppled and crashed down.

"Oh, man," gasped Axel. "We did it. We got away."

"TREE DIDN'T," said BEAST in a voice of deep sorrow.

"I'm sorry about the tree," Axel said. He hoped BEAST knew he meant it.

BEAST said nothing.

Axel checked the scanners to see where the Grabbem ships had gotten to. They were hovering high above, and now they were starting to move again.

"They're not giving up. We're going to need to hide."

There had to be a way to avoid the Grabbem scanners, but how? Agent Omega had said that if BEAST went deep underground, it would block the signal. Axel guessed the robot would be a good digger, but they didn't have time to tunnel through the earth.

Maybe if they couldn't go underground, they could go underwater. Now that was an idea he could get behind.

His excitement building, Axel steered BEAST away from the land and out toward the sea.

They flew above highways, parks and towns until the sea stretched ahead of them, a wide expanse of glittering water. Just as the Grabbem ships were coming close again, Axel brought BEAST down to the water's surface.

"BEAST, can you go under?"

"THIS IS NOT THE RECOMMENDED FORM FOR UNDERWATER MISSIONS," warned BEAST. "OTHER FORMS ARE AVAILABLE, BUT –"

"But I will need **apps** to access them, yes, I know! I don't care about the recommended form. Can you go under *now*?"

"YES."

That was all Axel needed to know. He tilted BEAST farther down.

There was a flurry of water as they dived through the surface, then everything was dark and quiet.

BEAST switched his eye beams on. Axel gasped.

A beautiful panorama opened up before them. They were surging down through the water, past shoals of glimmering fish and bright clusters of coral. The surface looked like beaten silver, rippling high above.

"Let's see those Grabbem creeps follow us down here," Axel laughed.

He steered BEAST over the edge of the drop-off and down into the deeper ocean. It was dark and cold down here, but BEAST's blue eye beams made the undersea world clearly visible. The jagged rocks and sandy seabed looked like an alien planet.

"This is amazing," he said.

"Spectacular view, isn't it?" said the voice of Agent Omega in Axel's ear.

CHAPTER 6

"Agent Omega!" yelled Axel. "You're alive!"

In his secret cupboard deep under Grabbem HQ, Agent Omega panicked as Axel's voice came **booming** out of his computer. He frantically turned down the volume. Then he waited to see if Axel's yell had attracted attention. His heart pounded in his ears.

No footsteps came.

He slowly turned the volume back up.

"Hello? You still there?" came Axel's voice.

"I'm here. I'm fine. Please talk *quietly*," Agent Omega said. He was wishing he'd thought to wear headphones.

"Okay," Axel whispered. "I'm fine, too. So is BEAST. We're hiding under the sea."

"Good thinking." Agent Omega smiled.

"What happened? I thought they'd detected you!"

"They almost did. Things were looking pretty hairy down here for a moment. I had to create an emergency to distract them."

"Emergency? What kind?"

Agent Omega glanced over to the thick plumbing pipe that ran from floor to ceiling in the corner of his room. He had taped a gadget to the side of it. "I used my emergency sonic destabilizer. It worked a bit too well, to be honest. I wanted to make a small flood in the computer lab, but ... well ... all the toilets on the research floor exploded."

"Wow!"

"The supervisor was furious. Partly because of the mess, partly because work got interrupted, but mostly because he happened to be **sitting** on one of the toilets at the time. But that's not important right now. I need to talk to you about –"

"Apps?" interrupted Axel.

Agent Omega gasped. "How did you know?"

"Let's just say I've had to learn a whole lot in the last thirty minutes."

"Fair point," admitted Agent Omega. "Okay. I'll make this as clear as I can. BEAST is a **shifter.** That means he can change his form to do different jobs."

Battle-Enabled Armored Shifter Transport, remembered Axel. "Yeah. BEAST said as much."

"Okay, you're up to speed. Now, the scientists here at Grabbem came up with a whole bunch of forms, each one suited to a different job they thought BEAST might need to do. Each form has an app. The app is kind of like the instructions to go into that form. With me so far?"

Axel nodded. "So BEAST is the hardware, and the apps are his software."

"Yes!" Agent Omega slapped his leg excitedly. "You've got it. Now, two very important things. Firstly, BEAST only has so many components to go around, so if an app gives him some kind of new ability, he'll probably lose some other ability to balance things out."

Axel thought about that. "So he could be a radio, or a toaster, but not a toaster-radio."

"Close enough. Also, the software to make BEAST change shape is pretty complicated. It takes up a lot of space in his brain. He can only store five apps at a time."

"Only five. Gotcha." Axel frowned as a thought struck him. "So if the apps are all made by Grabbem, and they don't want me to have them, how am I ever going to get any?"

Agent Omega grinned and leaned back in his chair. "Leave that to me, the master hacker."

He tapped a key on his keyboard. A window popped up on his computer screen: *sending*.

"BEAST?" said Axel. "Why are you, um, **vibrating?**"

"RECEIVING DATA!" said BEAST, sounding as happy as if he'd said *receiving birthday presents*.

Before Axel's eyes, five download bars appeared. Each one had a word next to it, which Axel guessed was the name of an app:

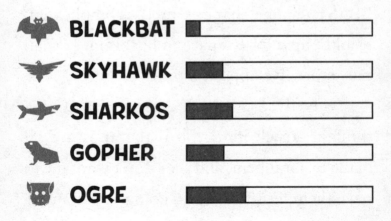

BLACKBAT

SKYHAWK

SHARKOS

GOPHER

OGRE

"So what do these apps do?" he asked.

Agent Omega rubbed his chin and coughed. "I, uh … to tell the truth, I'm not entirely sure. I think BLACKBAT is stealth mode, but the others? No clue. I hacked my way in and took what I could find. I figured any apps were better than none. You'll just have to work out what they do by yourself."

"No worries. Thanks, Agent Omega. I'm sure these will help us stay alive."

A red light on Agent Omega's computer began blinking furiously.

"Oh, no," he said. "They're on my trail again. I guess **exploding toilets** didn't slow them down as much as I'd expected. Come on, computer, hurry up and send those apps!"

The download bars crawled across Axel's vision, moving way too slowly.

Axel groaned. Why didn't an advanced robot like BEAST have a better roaming internet connection?

"Are those Grabbem ships still up there?" he asked BEAST.

"YES," BEAST told him. "AND ... **SOMETHING ELSE.**"

That made Axel jump. "What is it? Can you tell?"

"SORRY, AXEL. IT'S BIG, AND FLYING, AND IT SCARES ME."

Axel boggled. "Um. Agent Omega? A little help here? BEAST isn't making any sense."

"Oh yes, he is," said Agent Omega, sounding very grim. "Axel, I think I know what's up there with those Grabbem ships. And if I'm right, things just got a whole lot worse."

Gus Grabbem Junior sat in the cockpit of his very own fighter craft, playing deafening thrash metal music through the speakers.

The fighter was shaped like a slender dart with swept-back wings. Every bit of it was gleaming black, except for the tips of the missiles under the wings, which were red. Gus licked his lips. There were a *lot* of missiles.

Just for the sheer fun of it, he flew down low over a nearby town. The black fighter roared through the sky, so low down it looked like it must be crashing. People looked up, pointed and screamed. The force of the wind in its wake ripped tiles off rooftops.

A child's ice cream fell out of its cone and went **SPLAT** on the sidewalk.

Gus laughed and pulled the joystick back, climbing up into the sky. He turned down the thrash metal music and thumbed the communicator button: "Nearly there, Dad. I can see those **two losers** you sent out up ahead."

"Nice one, son," came the voice of Gus Grabbem Senior. "Did they get the robot yet?"

"Nah. They're just flying in circles over the sea."

"Ha! Never send an employee to do a Grabbem's job," sneered Gus Senior. "When they get back here, **I'll fire them.**"

"Can I watch?"

"Of course you can! But first, you take charge, son. Show those losers how it's done. Go bring that robot back. In bits if you have to."

"Oh, I'll smash it to bits all right," murmured Gus Junior. "No filthy common kid gets to steal *my* robot. I'd rather blow it up!"

CHAPTER 7

The downloads were almost complete. Only BLACKBAT was left. The bar crept slowly toward the end like a snail going back to school after the summer.

Agent Omega used his computer to scan through the Grabbem systems and found what he was looking for. Hangar thirteen, Gus Grabbem Junior's personal vehicle bay, was empty.

"Axel, listen. There's so much I still have to tell you, but there's no time. BEAST was originally built for a boy around your age."

"Oh. I guess that explains why the compartment I'm in is my size," said Axel.

"That boy's name is Gus Grabbem Junior," Agent Omega went on. "Son of the multi-bulti-billionaire who happens to be my boss. He's the most spoiled, violent, **disgusting** little brat you could ever hope to meet."

"Hey!" Axel said. "Stop that!"

"Huh?"

"If he's just a kid, you shouldn't say those things about him."

"... I beg your pardon?" Agent Omega boggled.

"Even if he's mean, you don't have to be mean, too," Axel explained. "And we don't know why he's like that. He might have good reasons. Maybe he's got family troubles or something."

Agent Omega angrily opened his mouth to yell at Axel, then decided he'd better not.

Calm down, Cedric, he told himself. *Axel's just a nice kid. He wants to see the good in everyone. He doesn't know what young Gus is capable of.*

But he was about to find out.

Something slashed down through the water just ahead of BEAST, leaving a foamy wake like a torpedo. Axel had just enough time to think, *What in the world could that be?* and then the explosion hit.

Underwater, it was somehow loud and muffled at the same time. A shockwave tore

BEAST upside down and smashed Axel hard against the cockpit's padding. They hurtled backward, cartwheeling, and slammed against a wall of undersea rock.

Axel struggled to turn BEAST the right way up. He could barely see anything at all in the clouds of sediment from the explosion. A few sad, ragged scraps drifted past his eyes. They looked like they had once been fish. The blast had cooked them in a split second.

A voice rang out from BEAST's speakers: "Hey, **weirdo!** This is Gus Grabbem Junior speaking. How are you doing down there?"

Axel had the funniest feeling he'd been in this situation before, somehow. "Can he hear me?" he asked BEAST.

"Of course I can hear you, **dill weed.** You're in *deep* trouble. You know that, right?"

There was a soft *ping*. Axel glanced over and saw that the apps had finally finished downloading.

A message from Agent Omega appeared underneath: **Can't talk more b/c GG may hear. Only way 2 kp BST safe: take out trackng device. Gd lk. O.**

"Gd lk to you, too," Axel whispered.

Gus sang in a neener-neener tone: "*You stole my ro-bot, and now you're going to pa-ay.*"

"I didn't steal him!" Axel yelled. "He ran away of his own free will!"

"**Bzzzt.** Sorry. Wrong answer. You lose. Good-bye."

When Gus said that, Axel knew what must be coming. He fired BEAST's rockets and roared up through the water, just in time for the next missile to whip down and hit the place where they'd been seconds before.

Another thunderous blast, another slam of water – but this time they were already moving, and it just pushed them forward all the faster.

Axel thought quickly. They couldn't stay down here, or Gus would just keep firing until he blew them out of the water. They were going to have to fight. He just hoped the apps would help.

Then he thought about how the crab ship's missile had **destroyed** a tree and how miserable BEAST had been about it. Somehow, they had to fight in a place where nobody would be hurt. Not even plants or animals, if Axel could help it. Those poor **cooked** fish ... But where could he go?

"You still down there, **Captain Garbage?**" mocked Gus.

Just like that, Axel had his answer.

"*Garbage*," he said softly to himself. "Of course. BEAST, I need you to fly as fast as you can."

"ROGER," BEAST said. "ENGAGING SUITABLE APP NOW."

One word lit up in brilliant blue: **SKYHAWK.**

Mechanical parts hummed and buzzed in BEAST's limbs. Axel felt an odd lurch as the cockpit changed shape, becoming more of a seat.

Then more words lit up in red: **Danger! Not for underwater use!**

"Oh, man," said Axel. "I should have thought of that. We need to get out of the water right now." He hit maximum thrust.

BEAST broke the surface like a rocket, water pouring off him, and tore up through the sky. As BEAST climbed, he *changed*.

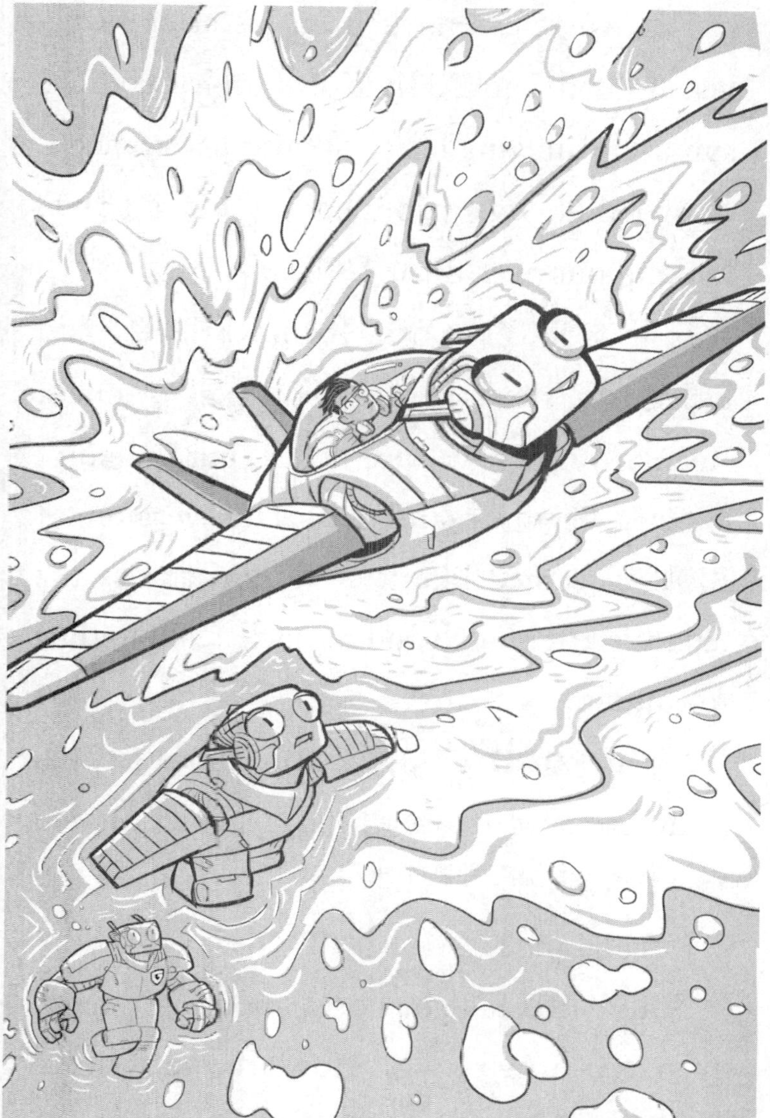

Flat wings extended from his arms as his legs folded back. His chest cavity rotated smoothly, moving his pilot onto his stomach. Now Axel was propped on his elbows, looking out over BEAST's head.

In his SKYHAWK form, BEAST had become a sleek jet fighter. Axel grinned. Regular BEAST was pretty fast, but he hadn't exactly been streamlined. This version of BEAST seemed like it could zip across the Atlantic after lunch and be back again in time for dinner.

"You **fool!**" Gus Grabbem screeched, and burst out laughing. "You picked SKYHAWK?"

"Yeah, and?"

"SKYHAWK's got no weapons. It doesn't even have arms or legs! How are you going to **fight,** huh?"

Axel remembered what Agent Omega had said about how BEAST's forms always lost some kind of ability as well as gaining new ones. Well, it didn't matter. All he needed right now was speed, and SKYHAWK had that.

"Who said anything about fighting?" he told Gus. **"Eat my dust."** And he shoved the throttle as far as it would go.

The flesh on Axel's face dragged backward from the sheer force of acceleration. The country below them was a green blur, the clouds a random scurry of blue and white.

He tried easing BEAST gently from side to side and found it was much easier than before. Piloting SKYHAWK felt as smooth and natural as playing a flight simulator.

He tilted them over to the right and kept going until SKYHAWK had completed a full barrel roll.

An odd sputtering sound and a flash of greenish light made him glance at the rear-view screen. Gus was chasing him. His own black fighter was way out in front of the more sluggish Grabbem crab ships. And he was firing. Rapid pulses of yellow-green energy peppered the air around them.

"Guess what the other problem with SKYHAWK is?" gloated Gus as Axel dodged and weaved out of the way. He just needed Gus to follow him for a little longer. The landmarks he was looking for should be showing up at any moment.

"I give up. What is it?"

"You'll find out!"

More volleys of cannon fire drilled through the sky, seeking their target. Axel banked hard, but was a second too late. One of Gus's shots smacked into the underside of BEAST's right-hand wing and punched right through it.

BEAST moaned in what sounded very much like pain.

Axel stared at the **blackened circle** Gus's shot had made, and at the sparking exposed wires that lay inside the hole, looking like burned spaghetti. There was a **sickening lurch** as BEAST wobbled violently. The controls wrestled themselves out of Axel's hands.

"You see now?" laughed Gus. "SKYHAWK may be fast, but its armor's paper-thin. And as for those fat old jets on the back of it? Guess what happens if I score a hit right in the middle of one!"

Axel didn't have to guess. He knew.

This version of BEAST had a weak spot – and Gus Grabbem Junior knew exactly where it was!

Agent Omega was right, he thought. "Wow. You really are a jerk."

Gus Grabbem laughed – and the next thing he said made Axel's blood run cold.

"Cry more, noob!"

CHAPTER

8

It's him, Axel thought. *Gus Grabbem is BAGGER_63! No wonder he could afford an elite Tankinator if his dad's a billionaire.*

"BEAST, talk to me!" he said. "Are you badly hurt?"

"THE DAMAGE IS ONLY MINOR," said BEAST.

"Yahoo!" squealed Gus behind him, an all-too-familiar sound. "Got that fat jet engine locked in my sights. You are going down!"

As Gus opened fire, Axel put BEAST into a **crash dive**, ducking out of the path of his shots.

Axel saw they were flying close to the place he'd chosen for his battleground. There was no mistaking the high wire fences all around it, nor the towering crane with its giant grabber. *"Junk City!"* he whispered.

Everyone from Axel's town knew about Junk City. It was the biggest junkyard for hundreds of miles around. Everything from old farm trucks to disused train cars ended up in one of its teetering piles.

The woman who ran Junk City called herself Rusty Rosie. She often worked with his mom and Axel liked her, though he was a bit scared of her, too. She had big muscles, tattoos and one eye that was all cloudy, supposedly from "a load of **flying sparks** off of the angle grinder." He hoped Rusty Rosie wouldn't be angry with him after what he was about to do.

Smoke trailed from BEAST's wing as they hurtled down toward Junk City. Axel could clearly see the stacks of rusting cars like weird skyscrapers in front of him. "I hope this works," he murmured. "BEAST, change to whatever form has the most armor."

"SHIFTING TO **OGRE**," said BEAST.

SKYHAWK's smooth wings folded away. Out came BEAST's arms and legs again, only now they were thick and hefty looking. Instead of the fingers BEAST had had before, there were fat fingerless hands like mittens.

With a **_wheeze_-crump** sound, BEAST's head popped into his body and then back out, now looking like a little domed turret with blue eyes shining from it.

OGRE was clearly a form built for heavy-duty work. Axel moved the arms and felt tremendous power in them. OGRE packed a punch, too! He could break holes in a wall with this form, and laugh at the bricks bouncing off his head. Gus Grabbem wouldn't be able to shoot holes in BEAST now!

Wait. Something else was different. Something very important. Axel couldn't put his finger on quite what it was, but a feeling of horror was growing in his stomach.

They fell down from the sky toward Junk City. BEAST was going fast. **Perhaps too fast**. Even with his thick armor, Axel didn't want to crash-land BEAST if he could help it. He squeezed the thruster throttle.

Nothing happened.

And *now* he realized what was different.

The roar of BEAST's rocket thrusters had completely stopped.

"BEAST, what are you doing? **Fire thrusters!**"

"I CANNOT," BEAST said. "SORRY, AXEL. THE OGRE FORM CANNOT FLY."

The feeling of horror that had been growing in Axel's stomach turned into a full-on panic attack. How could he have forgotten? All of BEAST's forms had disadvantages as well as new abilities. Obviously OGRE swapped the power of flight for immense strength and thick armor plating.

Could he change back to SKYHAWK again? No. They were seconds from impact.

Axel did the only thing he could think of. He curled BEAST up into a ball.

Rusty Rosie sat on a deck chair outside her trailer, reading last week's newspaper and eating fistfuls of Choc Pops cereal from the box.

She glanced up. Something was hurtling out of the sky. Something green and roundish. She paused in mid chew.

"Meteorite?" she said to herself. "Or aliens?" She brushed some Choc Pops off her lap. "Better not be aliens. I'm not having anything to do with them. I don't want anybody sticking probes in **me.**"

The thing was coming in low under the clouds. Rosie pondered its flight path and raised an eyebrow.

"Shoot. Whoever he is, he's about to come down in my yard. I don't recall giving him permission to do that."

She couldn't hear Axel screaming as BEAST flipped over and over, completely out of control. The next second, BEAST **crashed** into a stack of six cars and sent them flying across the junkyard.

Rosie sprang to her feet. She ran down the muddy paths that threaded their way through her kingdom, her bare feet splashing in oily puddles, and quickly found the spot where BEAST had landed.

BEAST had hit an old cream-colored delivery van, back first. He had hit so hard that the van was crumpled around him.

Rosie stared as BEAST tried to stand up. When he finally did, the entire van came with him, rising up behind like the shell of a tortoise.

"Ouch," said Axel. His voice emerged from BEAST's head, amplified and metallic.

"Axel? Axel Brayburn?" Rosie put her hands on her hips and laughed. "Boy, I thought you were an alien! Did your mom build you that robot?"

"I'll explain later, I promise."

Axel took another step. BEAST seemed sluggish and heavy. Was it because he was in OGRE form? Oh, no – it was because BEAST had a van wedged on his back. He **wriggled** from side to side, trying to get the van off.

"Allow me!" Rosie grinned. She clambered across the mounds of junk and made for the yellow grab crane she used to pick up old cars. She climbed into the cabin and turned the key. The engine sputtered into life.

Axel held still, bracing himself, as Rosie swung the grab over and expertly caught the mangled van in its jaws. A quick tug, and away it came.

Axel flexed BEAST's limbs. "Thanks!" he called.

"No problem, kid!"

A scream of jet engines from overhead told Axel that the Grabbem crew had caught up with them.

The next second, Gus Grabbem opened up with his fighter's cannons. Bolts of energy sizzled through the air as he approached, tracking across the mud, the heaps of ruined cars and trucks, and hammering into BEAST.

"Yowza!" yelled Rosie, hunkering down in her crane's cabin.

But with BEAST in OGRE form, the cannon fire was about as dangerous as heavy rain. It zinged harmlessly off his thick armor plating.

Gus came around for another run. Axel held up BEAST's hand like a shield, and a fresh hail of cannon fire pinged off his palm.

"You okay?" he asked BEAST.

"NO DAMAGE," BEAST said.

In his cockpit, Gus Grabbem snarled with rage. Fine. So the boy – whoever he was – had figured out how to use OGRE. Well, he was about to find out that even OGRE had its weaknesses.

"You two, get your grabs ready," he told Alpha One and Alpha Gold. "Pick that thing up and bring it with us. We'll cut it open back at my dad's lab!"

CHAPTER 9

Alpha Gold and Alpha One slowed down until they were almost hovering on the spot. They approached BEAST from opposite sides, steadily closing in on him. They were only a few feet above the mounds of rusting metal that made up Junk City.

From underneath their shells came grabbing pincers on long, flexible cables. They snapped in the air – **snap-snap** – in a way that made Axel feel **queasy** with fear.

"Don't worry, kid," said Alpha One. "We won't hurt you. We just want that robot you stole."

"I won't let them take you," Axel told BEAST.

"BUT HOW WILL YOU STOP THEM?" BEAST whispered.

"We're going to do what Agent Omega said. We're going to fight."

Axel took a step forward and slammed BEAST's foot down in an earth-shaking stomp. He raised BEAST's hand and beckoned, a **come-at-me-bro** gesture.

Alpha One snapped: "Fine. Let's get this over with." He shoved a lever and both his ship's grabbing pincers shot out. They caught BEAST under the arms and locked tight.

Alpha One grinned. This was going to be even easier than he'd thought. Even better, he would get all the glory for capturing BEAST himself. Alpha Gold wouldn't even get a look-in.

"Target secure," he said. "Airlifting him out."

Alpha One fired his rockets, expecting to hoist BEAST into the air. But Axel had other ideas. He hooked one hand through the window of a wrecked school bus that lay on its side, anchoring BEAST in place. With the other, he took hold of the cables that the grabbers were attached to.

He heaved with all of the strength BEAST's OGRE form could muster, and to his amazement, Alpha One went **sailing** through the air. Axel swung him around and around in circles as if he were a plastic toy on a piece of string.

"Hey, kid, cut that out!" yelled Alpha One. "You're making me feel sick!"

"You need a hand, bro?" said Alpha Gold, who was hovering nearby.

"I got this," Alpha One shouted, trying to regain control of his ship. Axel kept on spinning him around by the crab ship's own long arms.

"Only it looks kind of like the kid's winning," said Alpha Gold.

"Well, he isn't!"

Alpha One tried not to be sick inside his ship. He was whirling around and around like that time he'd been to the **teacup ride** at the fair and he'd thrown up on his date. This had all gone wrong extremely fast. He'd thought he had the robot, but now the robot had him, and he couldn't just let go because the robot had grabbed hold of his arms.

He clenched his teeth and struggled with his controls. "Listen, you little punk, you're coming with me."

"I don't think so," Axel said. "Does that ship of yours have an ejector seat?"

"Uh ... yeah, why?"

"Because I'm giving you until the count of three, and then your ship's going into that junk pile over there. If I were you, I wouldn't be in it when it does."

Alpha Gold said, "*Now* do you want help?"

"I'm fine!" shrieked Alpha One. "He's bluffing!"

"One," said Axel, and swung the crab ship even faster.

"Do you even know how much this ship is worth?" wailed Alpha One.

"Two," said Axel. The whizzing cables made a **thrum-thrum** sound.

"You're not going to do it, you haven't got the strength, you wouldn't dare … "

"Three."

Axel slammed the ship down hard, as if he were cracking a nut.

A fraction of a second before the ship smashed into the junk pile, its canopy flew off with a **sproing** and an ejector seat fired out. Alpha One flew through the air in a graceful arc. His parachute popped and he drifted gently down, only to get caught on one of the tall floodlights that marked the perimeter of Junk City.

"Whoaaaaa," said Alpha Gold. "He *did* do it."

Axel unhooked his arm from the school bus and pried the limp grabbers off BEAST. He turned to face Alpha Gold. "Now it's your turn. You going to threaten us, too?"

"I'm just doing my job," said Alpha Gold. **"Hold still!"** He lunged at BEAST with his own extending grabbers, but Axel lurched out of the way.

Alpha Gold bit his lip nervously. Young Gus Grabbem was circling the junkyard above them, watching everything that was going on. If this robot wasn't brought back to base like he wanted, Alpha Gold would be fired on the spot.

If he grabbed BEAST the same way Alpha One had, then he'd just get spun around and slammed into the junk pile, too. He had to do something clever. But what?

In his OGRE form, BEAST was tall and top-heavy. Alpha Gold's face broke into a slow grin. He knew just what to do.

With his ship's grabbers, he picked up a rusting car with no windows or wheels.

He backed his ship up a little way, then charged at BEAST and threw the car at the same time.

Axel yelled as the car hurtled toward him, flipping end over end. He flung BEAST's huge arms up to protect himself.

The car **crashed** into them and knocked BEAST over backward. As Axel struggled to stand up again, flailing around on his back like a beetle, Alpha Gold quickly caught hold of BEAST's feet.

"That's how you do it," he said to himself. **"In your face,** Alpha One. Watch and learn."

He reversed his ship. Poor BEAST was dragged across the bumpity junkyard on his back. His shiny green armor became filthy with mud, rust and old motor oil. He let out a low electronic moan.

Inside BEAST's cockpit, Axel was having trouble finding which way was up. He clutched at cars and objects as they went past, but couldn't reach them. He couldn't even fire the thrusters to get away because the OGRE form didn't have any. Strength and armor were all very well, but he badly needed some agility right now.

Alpha Gold flew backward through the yard, with BEAST dangling upside down below him. Axel tried to clutch at the annoying grabbers and pull them off, but BEAST couldn't bend enough in the middle in this armored form.

A shout rang out across the junkyard: "Oh no you don't!" It was Rusty Rosie, swinging her crane around. She'd had a lot of practice. The claw at the end went right where she wanted it to go.

With a deafening **clang**, Rosie's yellow industrial grab crane caught hold of BEAST's upper body. Rosie worked the controls of her crane and fought with Alpha Gold, pulling BEAST back and forth in a gigantic tug-of-war.

"Let go of the boy, you **hired thug!**" she yelled.

"Stay out of this, lady," bellowed Alpha Gold. He heaved back on his joystick and pulled BEAST as hard as he could. The steely cable of Rosie's crane stretched taut. The metal arm groaned and gave a ***pop-pop-pop*** sound of rivets coming loose.

Rosie bared her teeth. "You come to my yard, you better not start anything because you know I'm going to finish it."

Black smoke coughed from the crane's engine plate and a nasty sound of grinding gears came from deep inside the works, but Rosie kept on struggling.

"BEAST, we've got to do something," Axel gasped.

"I AM ABOUT TO BECOME **TWO HALVES**," announced BEAST. "WHEN THIS OCCURS, I WILL NO LONGER FUNCTION."

Axel quickly glanced at what Alpha Gold was doing. The crab ship was in full reverse, trying to reel BEAST in like a fisherman, while Rosie's crane – which was beginning to buckle – held BEAST fast. Something had to give.

If only there was some way to slip free of Alpha Gold's grasp ...

CHAPTER 10

The idea came to Axel in a flash. "BEAST, change back to your normal form!"

With many **whirs** and **thrums,** BEAST's armor plating folded away. His arms shrank back to normal size. And so did his feet. They slipped straight through Alpha Gold's grabbers.

Suddenly, Alpha Gold was hanging on to nothing – and he was still stuck in full reverse.

As BEAST flew one way, Alpha Gold flew the other. He shot backward at an impressive speed and **crashed** right into a teetering mountain of scrap.

Rusty Rosie's junkyard was a dangerous place at the best of times, with ancient rusty bits and pieces stacked high. More than once, some little impact – a junkyard rat leaping onto a car hood, a stray gust of wind, even a pigeon dropping something from high above – had triggered a landslide, bringing tons of metal debris down.

The junkyard was an accident waiting to happen, and now it had happened. Alpha Gold made a noise like a puppy's **squeaky-bone** as the avalanche of scrap descended on him. Junk thundered down on his ship's windshield: old microwave ovens, a chunky gray laptop from 1996, a toy stroller, a half-squashed shopping cart and finally a purple teddy bear with only one eye that had once been mounted on the front of a garbage truck.

The teddy bear slid slowly down the armored glass, leaving a greasy trail behind, and fell off with a plop. *I know just how you feel*, thought Alpha Gold.

His radio crackled. "Nice going, **genius**," said Gus Grabbem Junior.

"I'm fired, aren't I?" said Alpha Gold.

"Oh, you will be," said Gus, his voice rising to a scream. **"From a cannon!"**

Meanwhile, on the other side of Junk City, Axel was carefully landing BEAST in front of Rosie's crane, which was now bent out of shape.

Rosie sighed. "Guess that last tussle was too much for her. Shame."

"We could straighten her back out for

you," said Axel. "BEAST is pretty strong."

Rosie shook her head sadly. "Nah, son. Wouldn't help. Her gears are shot. Listen, you'd better get out of here. There's still one of those creeps around."

Gus Grabbem isn't ever going to stop, Axel thought to himself. *He'll keep on coming until BEAST is destroyed. Agent Omega said there was a tracking device inside BEAST, but I don't know how to get it out. Even if I had the tools, I don't have the knowledge. What am I going to do?*

Then an idea came to him. "He'll keep on coming until BEAST is destroyed," he repeated to himself. "Maybe that's the answer ... Rosie, I'm sorry to ask, but I need one more favor."

Rosie narrowed her eyes. "What's on your mind?"

Gus Grabbem Junior had never been in such a terrible mood in his entire life. Not even the legendary ten-hour tantrum he'd had when he was three years old, after his mom told him he couldn't have another entire birthday cake to himself, had come close.

"**Useless agents!**" he screamed. "**Rotten kid!** Who even is he? What kind of boy takes another boy's robot? If I knew who he was I'd **smash** his face in."

The trouble was, he didn't really know what to do next. He'd expected Alpha One and Alpha Gold to fly back up with BEAST in tow. But that hadn't happened.

"Hey," said Axel over BEAST's transmitter. "Gus, are you there? I need to talk to you."

"Go ahead, **dork**," said Gus.

"I'm really sorry. Your robot's broken.

I think I'd better give it back to you."

"Broken?" Gus screamed.

Axel's voice was a sad, raspy whisper. "Yeah. It … it got hurt pretty bad when your guy and the crane were pulling it from both ends. It's not even walking properly now. But you can fix it up, right?"

Gus reached up to the controls for his ship's camera system. He zoomed in as far as he could.

There was BEAST, climbing up on top of a mound of old sinks, bathtubs and kitchen counters.

He looked terrible. One of his legs was dragging limply behind him. Torn cables trailed from his limb joints like **spaghetti.** Bits of broken machinery stuck out of the cracks in his body.

"You stole my robot," said Gus through

clenched teeth, "then you broke my robot, and now you want to **give my robot back to me?**"

"Just come get it. I'm bored with it now, anyway," Axel said. "Turns out I don't need expensive toys like you do, BAGGER_63. I've got *actual skill.*"

Gus Grabbem Junior's pupils shrank until

they were tiny black pinpricks of pure fury. "*YOU!*"

"AX-MAN, in the flesh. See you in the *Tankinator Arena*, **loser.**"

Gus let out a scream. He put his sleek fighter into an attack run. With a single swipe of his hand he activated every single missile left in his stores.

Then he thumbed the **fire** button again and again until his thumb ached. Missile after missile dropped down, flared into life and shot through the sky.

Inside BEAST, Axel saw the missile warning light go on.

"MULTIPLE WARHEADS INBOUND," warned BEAST. "WE ARE BOTH ABOUT TO BE DESTROYED."

"I don't think so," said Axel.

He popped open BEAST's canopy, climbed

out and ran for all he was worth.

BEAST stood on top of the hill of junk, watching him go. He raised a hand as if to wave good-bye.

Up in his fighter, Gus was panting hard. He watched the shaky video camera image of BEAST standing there and waving. The kid had climbed out – sensible – and was running away.

Gus **frowned** as he got his first real look at the boy who had led him on such a chase today. He couldn't make out very much, but he could tell the kid had brown skin, dark hair and glasses.

"If I ever meet you again, online or off, you'll wish I hadn't," Gus hissed. "Nobody messes with me. I'm the **fastest** and the **richest** and the **best**."

He folded his arms behind his head, put on a pair of sunglasses and sat back to watch what was coming next.

It was all over very quickly. One moment BEAST was there. The next moment he wasn't.

KA-**BOOM!**

The missiles hit the junkyard one after the other, exploding with bright, delightful **ka-thooms** and showering the area with debris. It seemed to be raining metal.

Gus smirked. The reflected explosions danced across his sunglasses.

He only wished he could hear the kid crying at the death of the useless robot. As if Gus would ever take back a **broken** plaything. Who did the kid think he was? Some dirty *poor* boy?

After the last of the missiles had struck and only smoke clouds were left, Gus checked his scanner. There was no signal from the tracking device that had been inside BEAST. Good. That meant the robot had been blown to such tiny pieces that barely a trace of him was left.

Gus still felt a little curious, though. He wanted to see for himself. He brought his fighter down low over Junk City.

The smoke cleared. The junk pile was gone. Where BEAST had been there was nothing but a crater, blasted in the mud.

Satisfied, Gus turned around and headed for home.

Down below, Rosie put her arm around Axel. He looked up at the sky, with tears running down through the grime on his face, and watched the tiny dot that was Gus Grabbem vanish into the distance.

"He really did it," Axel said. "It's over."

CHAPTER 11

The two of them stood together in silence for a moment. Eventually Rosie said, "I think it's safe to look now."

Axel immediately ran for the crater the missiles had made. He scrambled over the edge and looked down into it. His heart gave a sickening **thump.** There was no sign of BEAST at all.

"BEAST, can you hear me?" he yelled. "Did it work?"

From deep underground came a muffled, robotic voice.

"DARK ENVIRONMENT DETECTED. ENGAGING NIGHT-VISION MODE."

Axel let out a **wild laugh** of pure joy. He searched the smoldering crater for the tunnel opening he now knew had to be there. Rosie pointed it out to him – a hole as wide across as an elevator shaft, but half-hidden under an old disused army truck with no wheels that had landed on top of it.

Axel peered in. Deep at the bottom of the shaft, two steady and unblinking blue eyes looked up at him.

"Hang in there, buddy," he said. "We're on our way."

BEAST nodded.

"BEAST KNOWS. BEAST IS NOT AFRAID," he said.

As last-minute plans go, it had been a bit of a **desperate gamble.** Axel hadn't been sure that Gus Grabbem would take the bait. Luckily, the boy was every bit the spoiled, tantrum-throwing brat that Agent Omega had warned Axel about.

Maybe one day, Axel thought, he'd find out what had made the boy turn out so bad; but that was something to worry about another time.

The tricky bit had been making Gus think BEAST had been completely destroyed. Axel had remembered that the tracking device wouldn't show up if BEAST was far enough underground. So BEAST had shifted into **GOPHER** form – just as Axel had expected, it was a specialized tunnel digger – and had dug his own escape tunnel in a matter of minutes.

Then, just to make sure BEAST looked damaged beyond repair, they'd stuffed some broken cables and other bits of scrap into the cracks of his body. Rosie's junkyard had provided all the props they could ever need for that job.

"You'll only have about **half a second** to jump down the tunnel before the missiles hit," Axel had said. "Are you sure you can make it?"

"NO," BEAST had said.

Pretending to abandon BEAST and run away had been the hardest part. But now, as he looked down into his friend's shining eyes, Axel knew he would never have to abandon him again.

There was just one more job left to do.

It was cramped and uncomfortable at the bottom of the shaft, and it smelled of dirt, like a freshly dug garden. The only light was from a greenish bulb that Rosie had lowered down on a cable. But if they went back up to do this, the Grabbem forces would detect them. It had to be done underground.

Rosie lowered her welding mask and sparked her cutting torch alight. She turned the knob and the flame went from a yellow tongue to a brilliant blue-white spike. Axel held on to one finger of BEAST's enormous hand.

BEAST's chest plate had been removed. It had taken a long time. Now his systems lay exposed, as if he were having surgery.

Axel held his breath as the torch bit into a protective box. A smell of burning metal filled his nostrils.

BEAST trembled. Axel tightened his grip. The careful cutting went on. A **sizzling, spitting** noise filled the little cave.

"Well, that's as much as I can do, mate," said Rosie, wiping sweat from her forehead and flicking the torch off. "Sorry. I told you, I'm a scrap merchant, not a mechanic."

"Sounds like my cue," said Nedra Brayburn, stepping into the light. "Okay, BEAST. Keep as still as you can. I'll get this nasty little thing out of you in a jiffy."

"THANK YOU, AXEL'S MOTHER," said BEAST.

Axel was too full of emotions to say anything. There wasn't a mechanic like his mom in the whole world. She'd set off in her car for Junk City as soon as he'd phoned her and asked for her help.

He watched her clever fingers go to work inside BEAST's chest, snipping wires delicately and plugging in devices to keep BEAST stable. Then, very gently, she reached deep inside.

Slowly, she drew a black disk about the size of a watch battery out of the cavity in

BEAST's chest. "Easy now ... steady does it ... *gotcha!*" She held it up triumphantly. "One tracking device. BEAST, would you like to do the honors?"

BEAST gripped the disk in his fist and clenched. There was a short, sharp **crack.** Then everybody breathed a sigh of relief.

"That takes care of that," Nedra said.

BEAST tapped the Grabbem Industries logo on his chest. "CAN YOU FIX THIS, TOO?"

"Oh, I'd be glad to," said Nedra. "Hold still."

As she bent to work again, Axel said, "Nobody owns you, do they, BEAST?"

"BEAST BELONGS TO BEAST NOW," said the robot, quietly.

With a few quick swipes of the angle grinder and a dab of paint, Nedra turned the

G on BEAST's chest into a **B.**

"Like it?" she asked.

"YES. VERY, VERY, **VERY** MUCH."

"So, Rosie," said Nedra. "Dinner at our place on Wednesday night?"

"Sounds good to me," grinned Rosie.

"I'll cook," Axel said quickly. "I'll do **samosas.** To say thanks."

Rosie raised an eyebrow. "He cooks? You're bringing that boy up right."

Nedra shrugged. "I do try. I'm pretty pleased with how he's turning out."

"SO AM I," said BEAST.

CHAPTER 12

Silent as a ghost, BLACKBAT flew toward Axel's home.

BLACKBAT, as Agent Omega had guessed, was a **stealth-mode** form. It morphed BEAST into a bat-like shape with wide, flat wings and long ear antennae.

It wasn't as fast as SKYHAWK and didn't have any weapons, but it had amazing scanners. Axel could detect every creature within miles. Using the heat detector, he watched a cat scampering through bushes in the park, its body glowing orange. Its paw prints marked the path it had come along. He could even see a **tiny mouse** cowering not far away. *Don't worry, mouse,* Axel thought. *I won't let the cat know you're there.*

Even better, BLACKBAT was almost undetectable. It could sense other things, but other things couldn't sense it. It was invisible to radar, and used a special stealth field so that it blended in with its surroundings. During the day you might spot its shadow, or see a ripple in the sky where it was passing, but at night BLACKBAT could glide right over your head and you would never know.

"Good work back there," said Agent Omega, through the speakers. "Grabbem don't suspect a thing. They won't come after you."

"Glad to hear it," Axel said. His mom would be glad, too, he knew. She wanted them safe.

"Of course, you can still go after them, if you want," said Agent Omega slyly.

"What do you mean?"

"There are hundreds of Grabbem operations out in the world. **They're bad people,** Axel. Greedy, destructive and cruel. They destroy nature and take away people's homes just to make themselves rich. What's worse, they keep getting away with it."

Axel thought about that. Grabbem were basically bullies, and he didn't like bullies.

"What do you think, BEAST? Shall we keep fighting Grabbem?"

"TOGETHER?" said BEAST.

"Always."

"BEAST WILL FIGHT."

"We're in," said Axel.

"Sounds good to me," said Agent Omega. "I'll be in touch soon. Listen, I'd better go. Looks like your mom's calling."

A message flashed up on BEAST's display. **Incoming call: Nedra Brayburn.**

BEAST had one other feature Axel hadn't known about. They'd found it when Rosie had removed BEAST's chest armor: a phone slot.

Axel's phone clicked right in as if it had been meant to go there. Now he could make calls or send messages from inside BEAST with voice commands. And other people could call him, too.

"Hi, Mom," Axel said.

"Are you nearly home yet?"

Axel laughed. "I *am* home. I can see you in the driveway." He could, too – a tiny figure staring up at the sky.

"Well, I can't see you!"

Axel swept in to land in front of her and switched BEAST to standard form. Nedra yelped and jumped backward.

"Get inside quick before someone sees you," she urged. **"For Pete's sake.** There's enough explaining to do as it is!"

Later, as they ate pizza around the kitchen table, Nedra glanced up at BEAST looming over her son. "He can't stay in this house, Axel. You understand that, right?"

"I know," Axel sighed.

"So I was thinking … he has a digging form, right? Maybe he could dig you a cave under the house. A **secret lair,** kind of thing."

"Awesome idea!" Axel leapt to his feet and

gave her a hug. "And maybe after BEAST has finished digging us a hideout, you and I can go for a walk. Or something."

"Outside?" Nedra asked.

"Yeah. We should get out more, you know. It's nice out there."

"You wouldn't rather stay in and play games?"

Axel laughed. "Not today. Come on, BEAST. Let's get to work!"

THE END
(for now)

ABOUT THE AUTHOR & ILLUSTRATOR

ADRIAN C. BOTT is a gamer, writer and professional adventure creator. He lives in Sussex, England, with his family and is allowed to play video games whenever he wants.

ANDY ISAAC lives in Melbourne, Australia. He discovered his love of illustration through comic books when he was eight years old, and has been creating his own characters ever since.